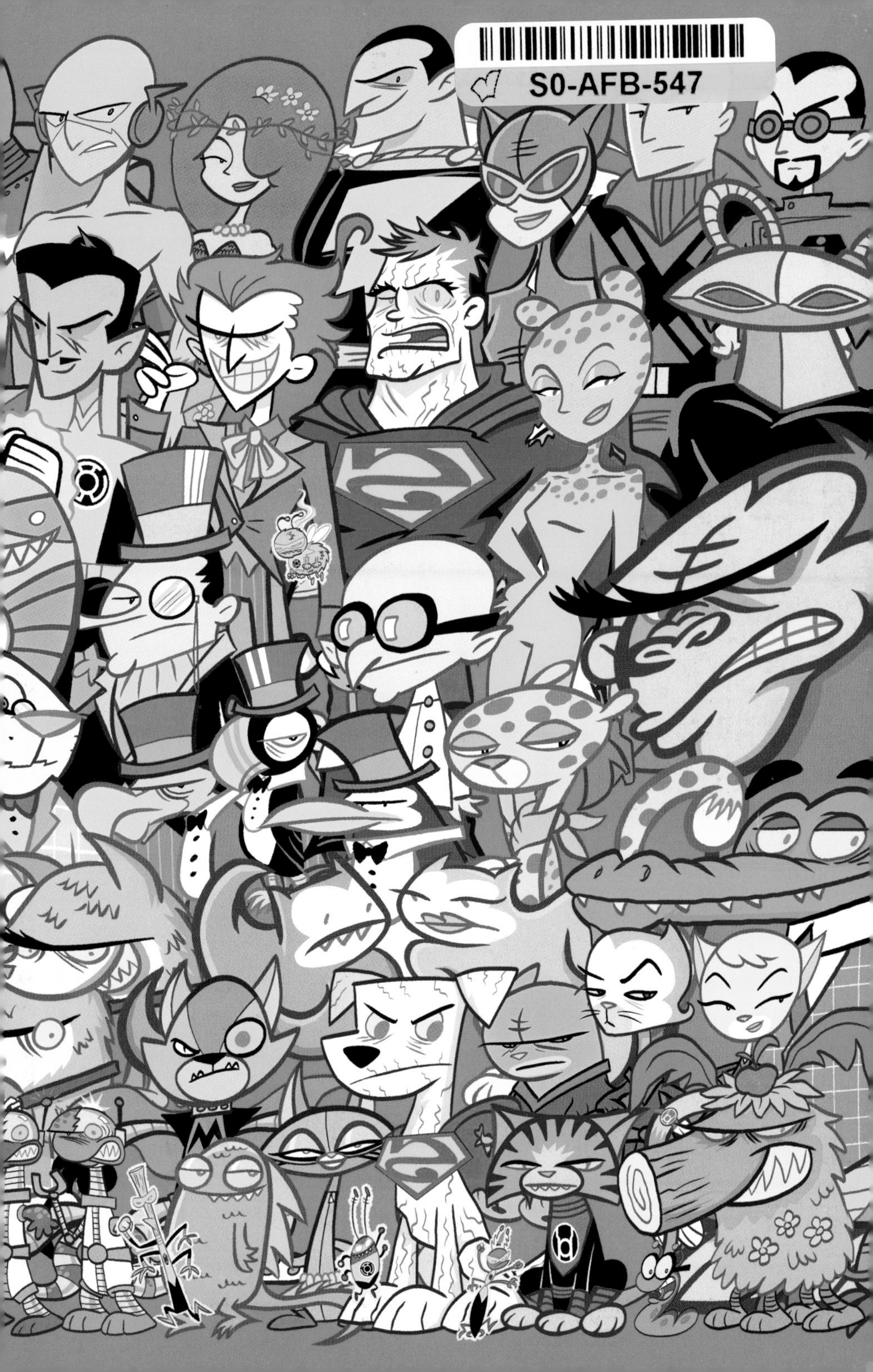

DC™ SUPER-PETS!

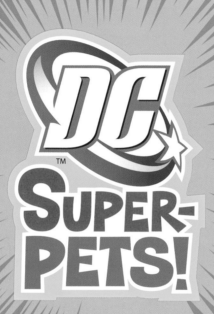

by Sarah Hines
Stephens

SUPERPOWERED PONY

illustrated by
Art Baltazar

Superman created by
Jerry Siegel and Joe Shuster

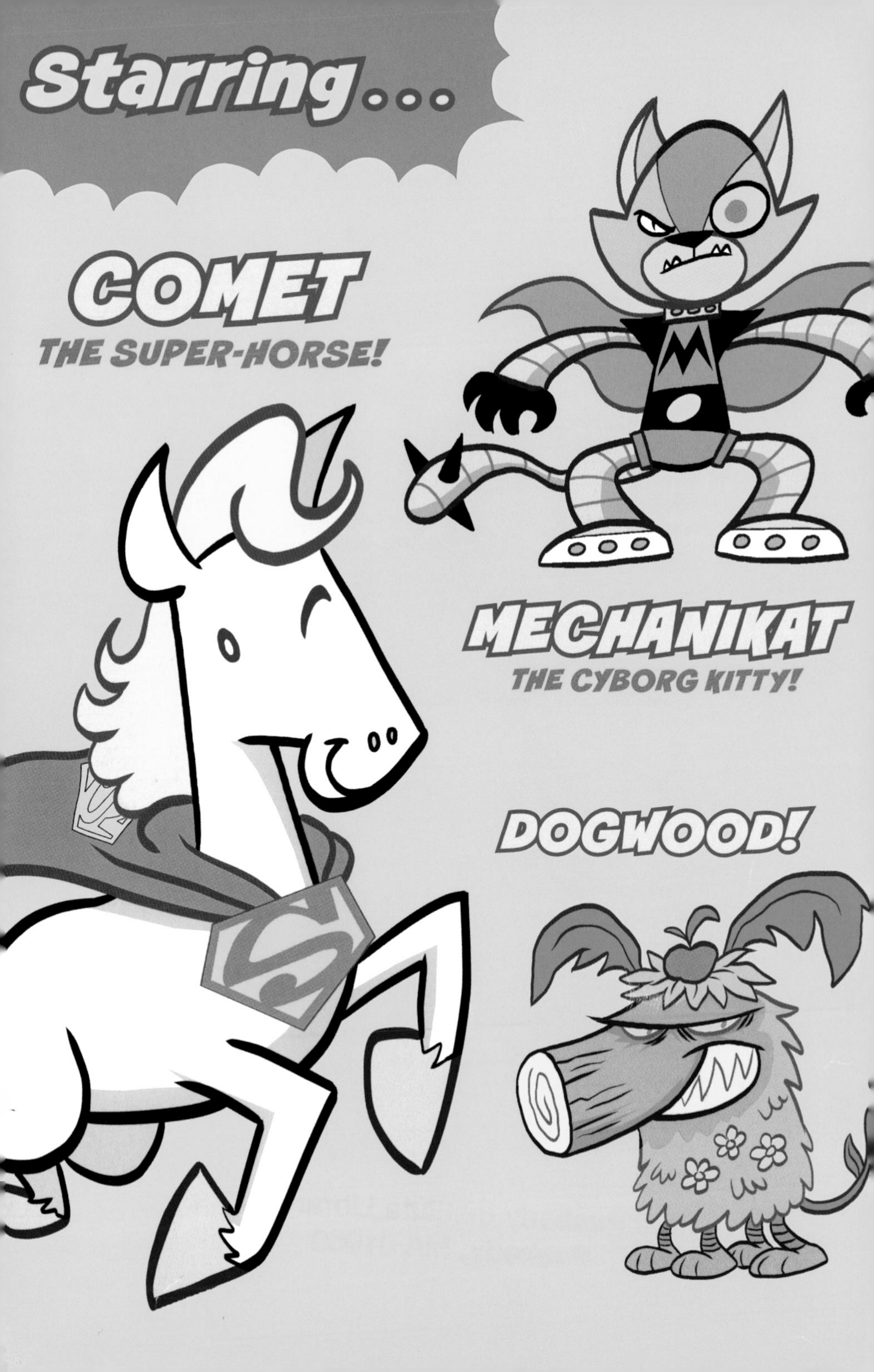
Starring...
COMET
THE SUPER-HORSE!
MECHANIKAT
THE CYBORG KITTY!
DOGWOOD!

TABLE OF CONTENTS!

SUPER-PET HERO FILE 002 :
COMET

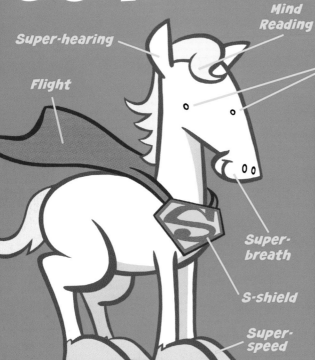

Mind Reading

Super-hearing

Heat & X-ray Vision

Flight

Super-breath

S-shield

Super-speed

Super Hero Owner:
SUPERGIRL

Species: Super-Horse

Place of birth: Greece

Age: Unknown

Favorite Food: Oatmeal cookies

Bio: An ancient spell gave Comet the same powers as the Girl of Steel and her family.

Super-Pet Enemy File 002:
MECHANIKAT

- X-ray Vision
- Kryptonite Chamber
- Mace Tail

Super-villain Owner:
METALLO

Super-Pet Enemy File 002B:
DOGWOOD

- Plant Control
- Super-smell
- Camouflage

Super-villain Owner:
POISON IVY

Chapter 1

FELINE FORCE

In the shadows of an airplane factory, **Mechanikat** sat and licked his paws. The evil kitty was a cyborg. He was half animal, half machine. He had the sharp claws and teeth of a cat. He also had the power, strength, and metal shell of a robot.

No creature would dare make him angry. But Mechanikat was already a very, very furious furball!

The sourpuss looked around the room. Dozens of cats and kittens were busy building robot soldiers.

With his **feline eye**, Mechanikat
saw the workers fumbling with
tools and moving slowly. With his
mechanical eye, the cyborg looked
inside the machines with X-ray vision.

Mechanikat spotted what was wrong with the new robots. Each contained loose bolts, missing pieces, and crossed wires. His Feline Force looked like a pile of scrap metal.

"Hiss!" The cyborg spat sparks. He arched his back. He yowled at the slow workers. **"Get out! Get out!"** the cat shouted. **"You are all fired!"**

More sparks flew. Mechanikat sank his claws into the floor.

"Meow!" the worker cats screamed. They ran to get away. They didn't want to stick around and see what Mechanikat would do next.

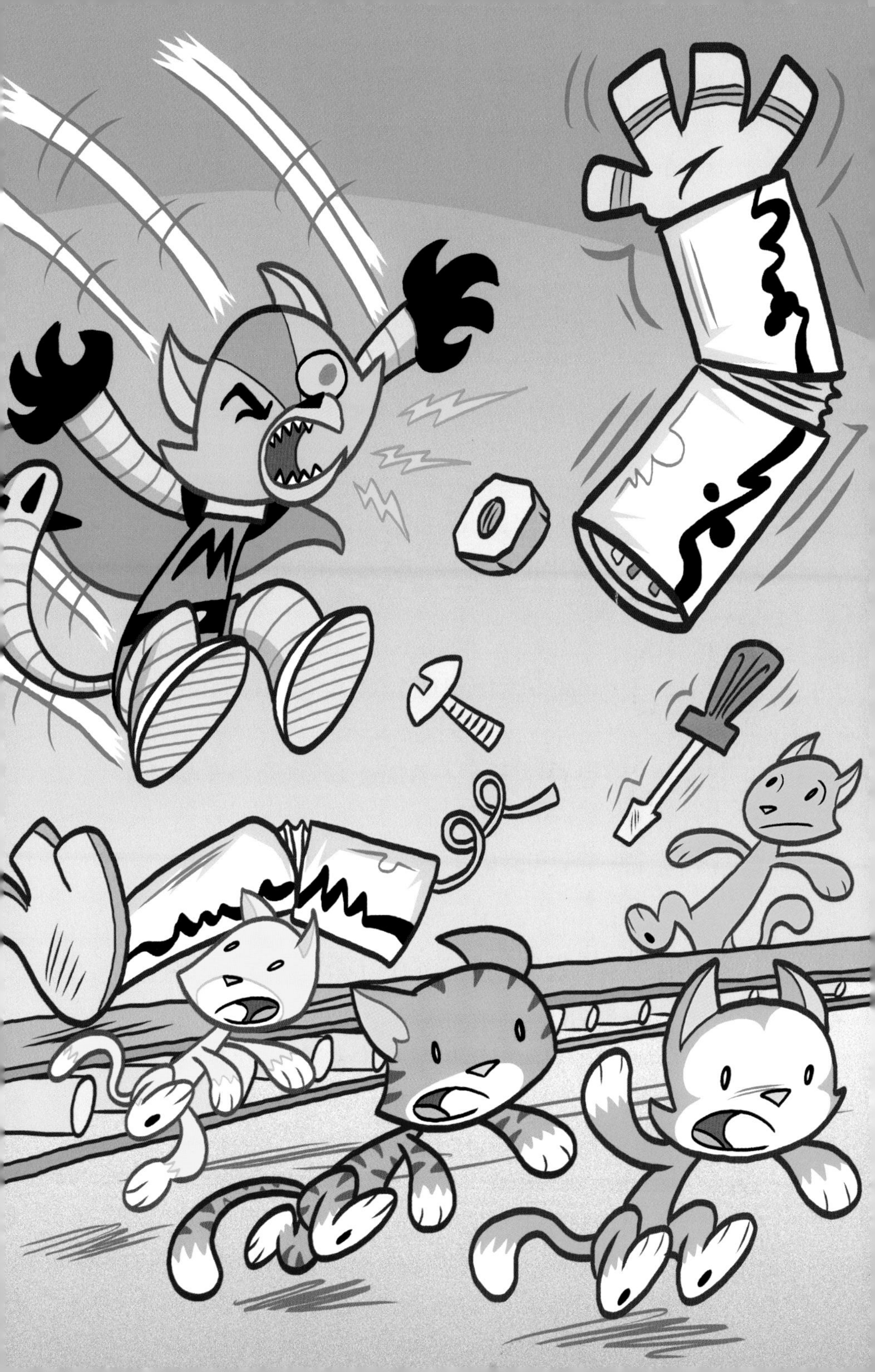

As the worker cats sped out of the factory, Mechanikat paced the floor. **SKREECH!** His front claws scraped against the concrete.

BLAM! BLAM!

His metal feet landed with loud clangs. **He didn't know what he was going to do now.**

The worker cats had been doing a terrible job. They were slow. They argued. They took lots of naps. But now, Mechanikat had no one.

The evil cyborg needed workers who could build quickly. **Krypto the Super-Dog** and the rest of the **Legion of Super-Pets** were busy protecting the universe. Mechanikat needed the Feline Fighting Force finished before his enemies returned to Earth.

Until the heroes arrived home, Mechanikat had a great opportunity. Without the Super-Pets to stop his plans, he could fulfill his dream.

He could create a *purrrrfect* world!

Mechanikat closed his eyes. The gears in his head turned. The villain thought about the Earth after he had finally taken over. He pictured a fish in every food bowl, humans as servants, and dogs behind bars.

Mechanikat hoped these dreams would soon be real, but time was running out. He needed to find workers who were friendly and loyal.

With a swish of his spiked tail, Mechanikat walked out of the factory.

"Ruff! Ruff!" A strange bark stopped Mechanikat's thoughts.

In a nearby park, the canine villain **Dogwood** chased a stick. He waited for his owner, **Poison Ivy**, to return.

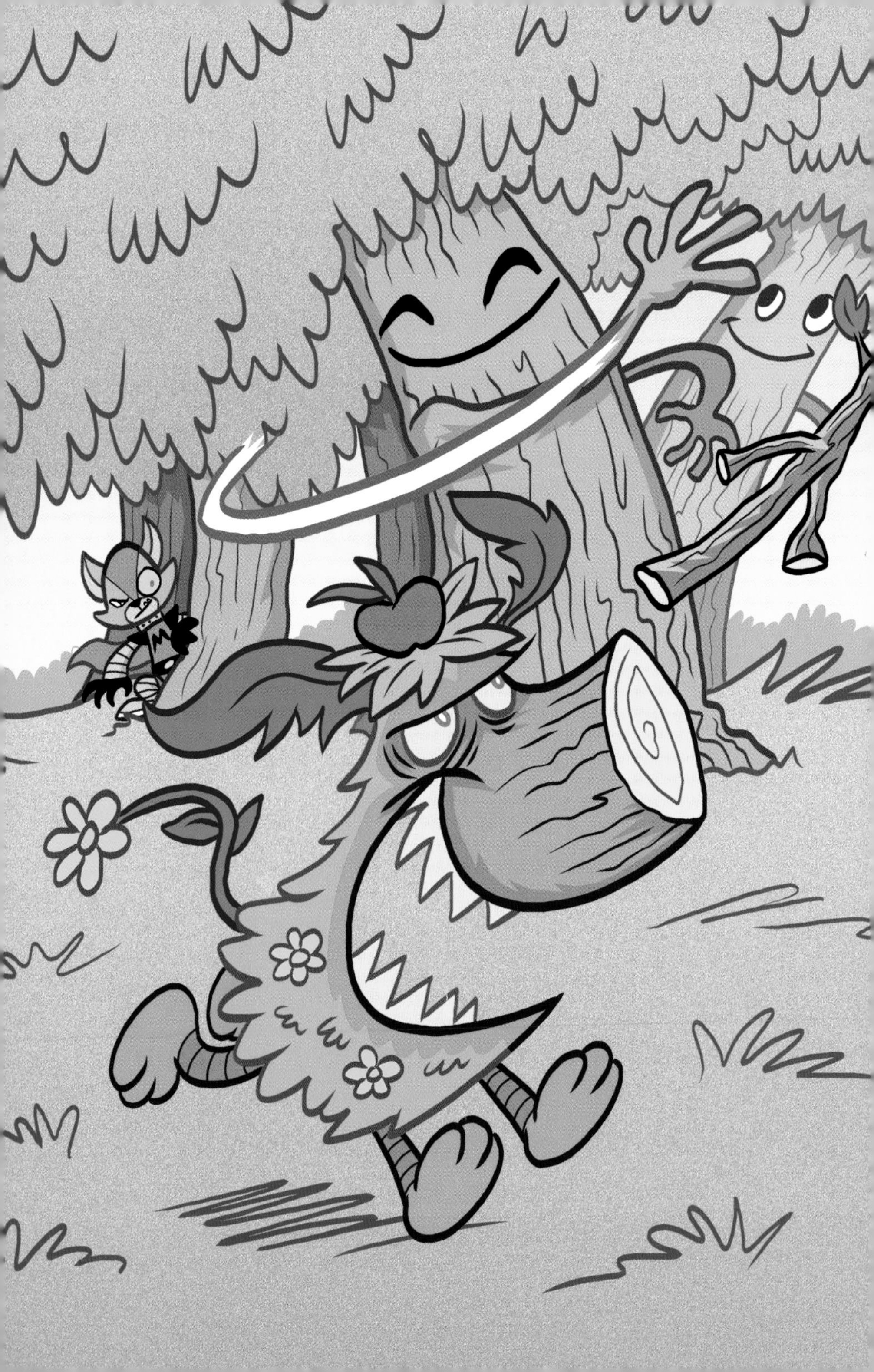

Mechanikat watched. The odd dog ran through the grass, picked up the twig, and took it back to a tree.

Dogwood was half plant himself. He had the power to control other plants with his mind! At the moment, he was using the tree to play fetch. The tree wrapped the end of one hanging branch around the stick and threw it again and again. FWIP! FWIP!

Mechanikat's robot eye twitched. Watching Dogwood had given him a wonderful — **and horrible** — idea.

Chapter 2

PLANT WORKERS

Mechanikat walked slowly toward Dogwood. The green dog stopped playing fetch. Cats did not approach him very often.

"We're a lot alike," Mechanikat said. "I am half machine and half animal. You are half animal and half plant."

HUFF! HUFF! Dogwood panted.

"Neither of us has any need for humans," Mechanikat continued.

Dogwood did not disagree. By controlling plants to help him find food and throw sticks, he had all he needed. Of course, Dogwood did get lonely sometimes. Luckily, the canine had discovered that shrubs were good at scratching him behind the ears.

"Is it true you can control any plant?" Mechanikat asked.

"**Yup,**" Dogwood said. His tongue nearly wagged against the ground.

"Is it true you can control many of them at once?" Mechanikat asked.

"**Uh-huh,**" Dogwood said.

"That's amazing!" Mechanikat said. He was trying to make friends with the plant pup. "Could you control this whole meadow of grass?"

"**Sure,**" Dogwood said, scratching his ear with his back leg. "**If I had a reason to do it.**"

Mechanikat smiled. "Well, my friend, close your eyes," he purred into Dogwood's ear. **"Picture a world where your bowl is always filled with —"**

"Dog biscuits?" Dogwood barked.

Mechanikat cringed. **"Yes,"** he said. **"And you spend all your days —"**

"Fetching balls?" Dogwood yipped.

"Delightful," Mechanikat continued. "There will be no leashes, no kennels, no signs saying 'Keep Off the Grass.'"

"No leashes!" Dogwood nodded.

"This world could be mine — I mean, ours. A _purrrrfect_ world. For both of us," said Mechanikat. "All you need to do is ask your plant friends to come work for me . . . **if you can."**

"I can! I can!" Dogwood replied, wagging his tail wildly. He jumped to his feet. "Watch me! Watch me!"

Dogwood stood. A moment later, a gust of wind whipped through the park. WHOOSH!

Then suddenly, the long blades of grass pulled themselves up by the roots. They began to march!

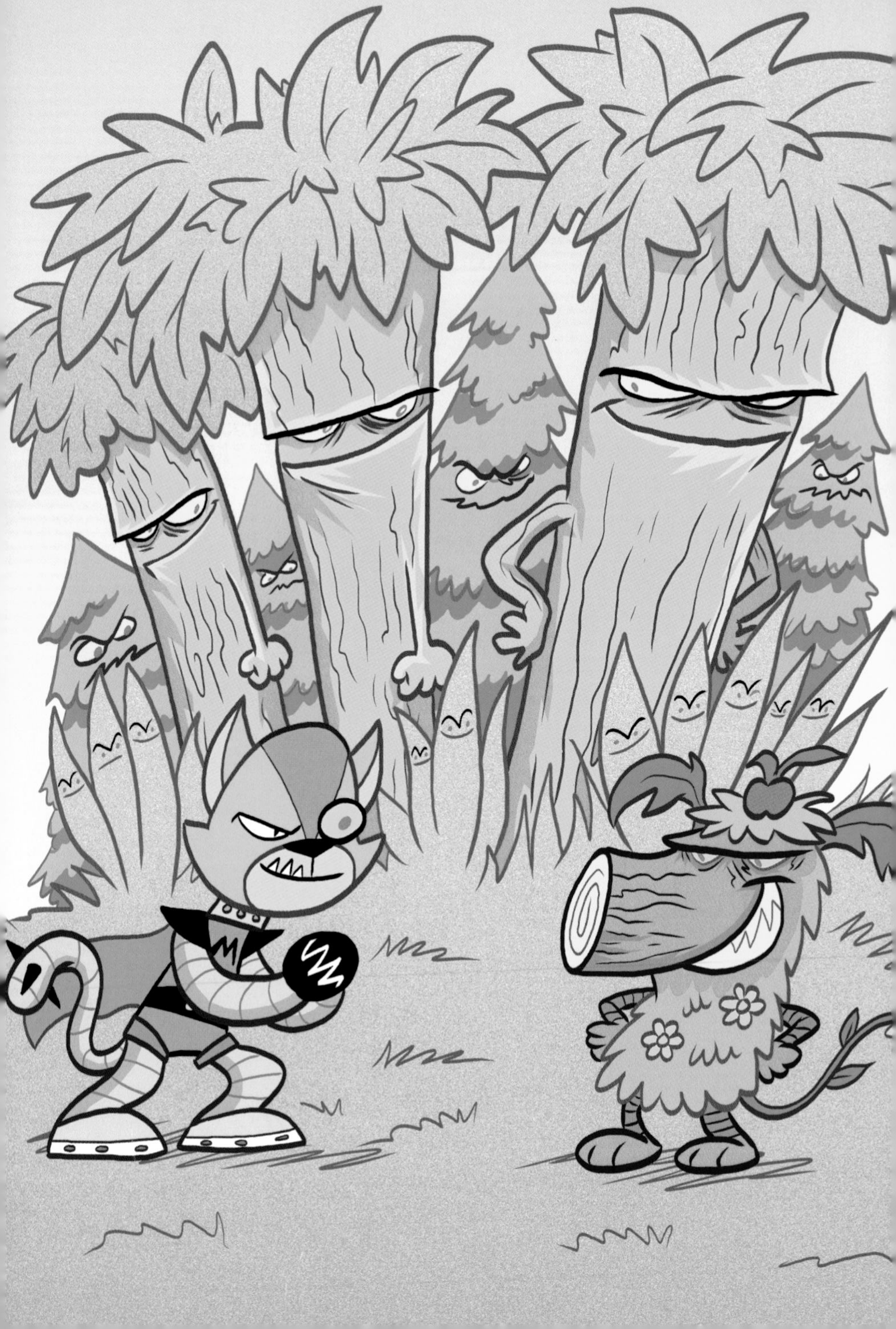

"**How's that?**" Dogwood said. He looked at Mechanikat with pride.

"**That's a good boy,**" Mechanikat answered. "But how about those trees?" He pointed to the nearby forest.

Dogwood aimed his nose. A sudden breeze exploded across the area.

Trees ripped out of the ground. They circled the villains and awaited orders.

Mechanikat yowled. The plan was working better than he had dreamed.

Within moments, Mechanikat was leading a jungle of plant life toward the factory with Dogwood at his heels. Their army awaited.

RUFF! RUFF!

When the doors to the factory opened, Dogwood barked in alarm. He saw the shiny metal faces inside.

"This is my Feline Fighting Force," Mechanikat explained. "Don't worry. They'll fight for canine-kind, too. **But only if your plants will help build them!**"

Dogwood got his plants working right away. They used their leaves like hands. They used their vines to hold screws in place or reach into tight spaces. In a short time, half of the Feline Force was fit to fight.

Meanwhile, **Comet the Super-Horse** was flying above Metropolis. He was on his way to meet his owner, **Supergirl**, at the Fortress of Solitude.

Suddenly, something caught Comet's eye. The usually green parks of the city were nothing but brown dirt. The trees, grass, flowers, and vines were all gone!

Something was very wrong.

Comet flew down for a closer look.

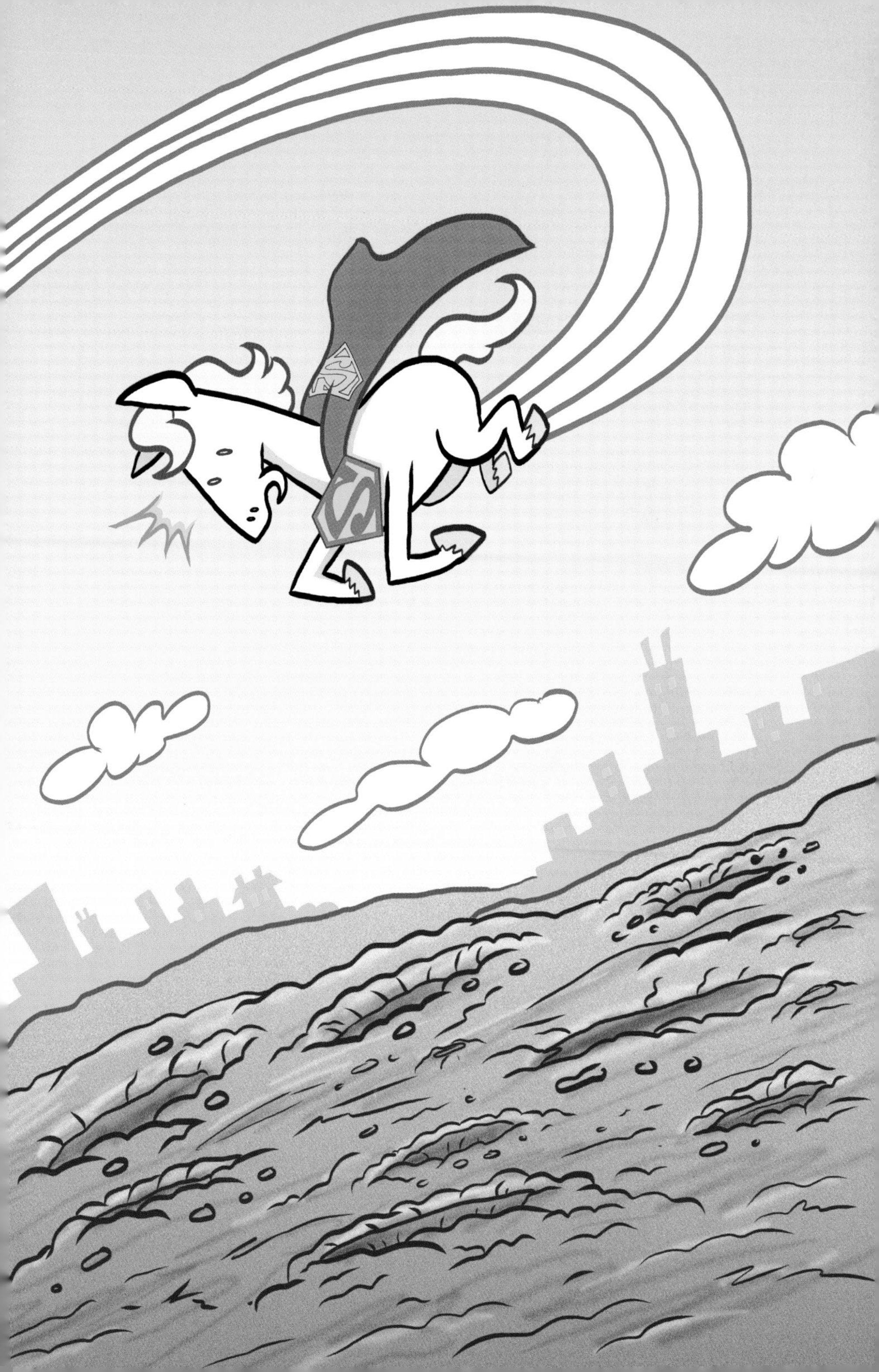

"**Neigh!**" Comet snorted. He pawed the ground. The rest of the **Super-Pets** were out of town. The superpowered pony would have to investigate the missing plants on his own.

Comet closed his eyes. His powers allowed him to read the minds and thoughts of others. Pictures flooded his brain until the one he wanted stuck.

In his mind's eye, he saw a troop of plants working in a dark factory. The plants were wilting without sun, water, and soil.

They were working hard. The army

they were building looked dangerous.

WHOOOSH!

Once again, Comet took to the skies!

The Super-Horse sped toward the factory. He peeked through a crack in the door. The pictures Comet had seen in his head were now right in front of him. The huge army of deadly cat-bots was growing bigger every second.

The masterminds behind the evil army were there, too. **Dogwood kept a watchful eye on the plants. Mechanikat snoozed in his office.**

A quick peek into the evil cat's dreams told Comet all he needed to know. He was double-crossing the dog!

Once his army was built, the feline villain had terrible plans for the pup. **However, Comet had no plan for letting Mechanikat get that far.**

With the cat-bot army growing every second, there wasn't a moment to lose. Comet turned and kicked in the door.

KRAAAAAASH!

Spotting the Super-Horse, Dogwood signaled his green team. The plants left their workstations. They faced the powerful horse. Using nuts and bolts as ammo, they began to fire at Comet.

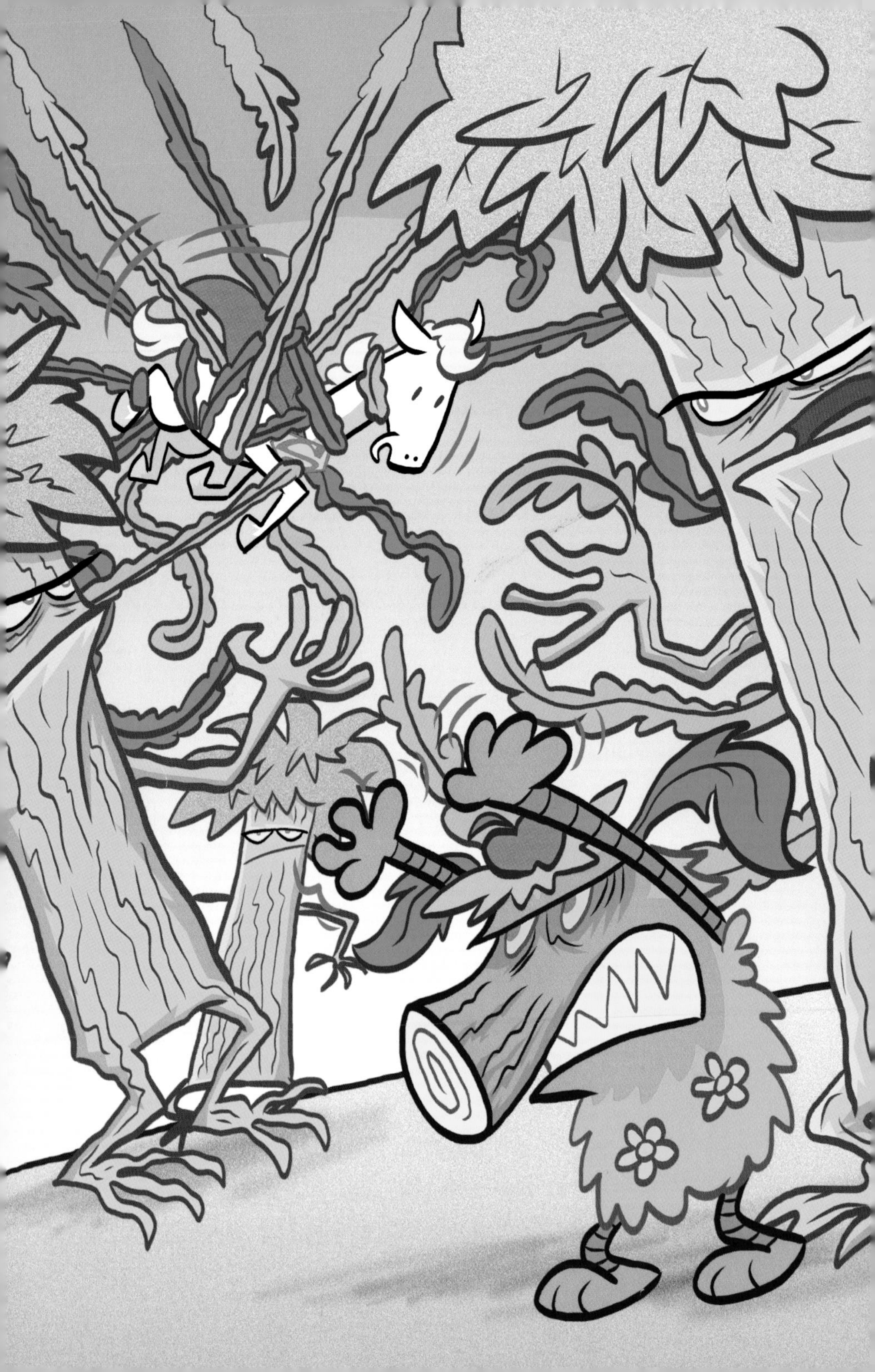

Comet dodged the hardware. Then he kicked at the grass with his hooves. One of the vines wrapped around his legs, but he snapped it off with his super-strength.

As Comet continued fighting off the plants, he turned and looked at Dogwood. **"A dog working for a cat!"** the Super-Horse said. **"I never thought I'd see the day."**

The hair on Dogwood's back stood straight up. "I'm not working *for* him," he growled. "I'm working *with* him."

"That's not what he thinks,"

Comet said. He nodded toward the office where Mechanikat slept. "That cat would never share any of his power with a dog. In fact, he plans to lock every dog on the planet into the world's largest kennel. But only after he's gotten you to do his dirty work."

Dogwood whimpered and frowned.
The plants attacking Comet suddenly stopped moving. The Super-Horse had gotten through to the bad dog.

But the fight was not over yet.

 Mechanikat

threw open the door to his lair. He

had woken up from his catnap to see

Comet in his hideout. The red "S"

hanging from Comet's neck short-

circuited Mechanikat's clockwork.

Even more than humans, the crazy cat could not stand Super-Pets or their Super Friends.

"What's thissssss?" the cyborg hissed at Dogwood. Then he noticed that Dogwood's veggie friends were standing still. **"Make those leafy monsters get back to work!"** he shouted. "I'll take care of the horse."

Dogwood dropped his head. The leaves on the plants fluttered, and the green team shuffled slowly back toward the cat-bots.

Dogwood did not make a sound as he watched them return to their work.

Comet was stunned. He thought he had gotten through to the plant pooch. But Mechanikat's control was too powerful!

"Thought you could ruin my plans?" the evil cat asked.

FWOOOOSH!

With a mighty leap, Mechanikat launched himself onto Comet's back. He sank his metal claws into the horse's thick skin and hung on.

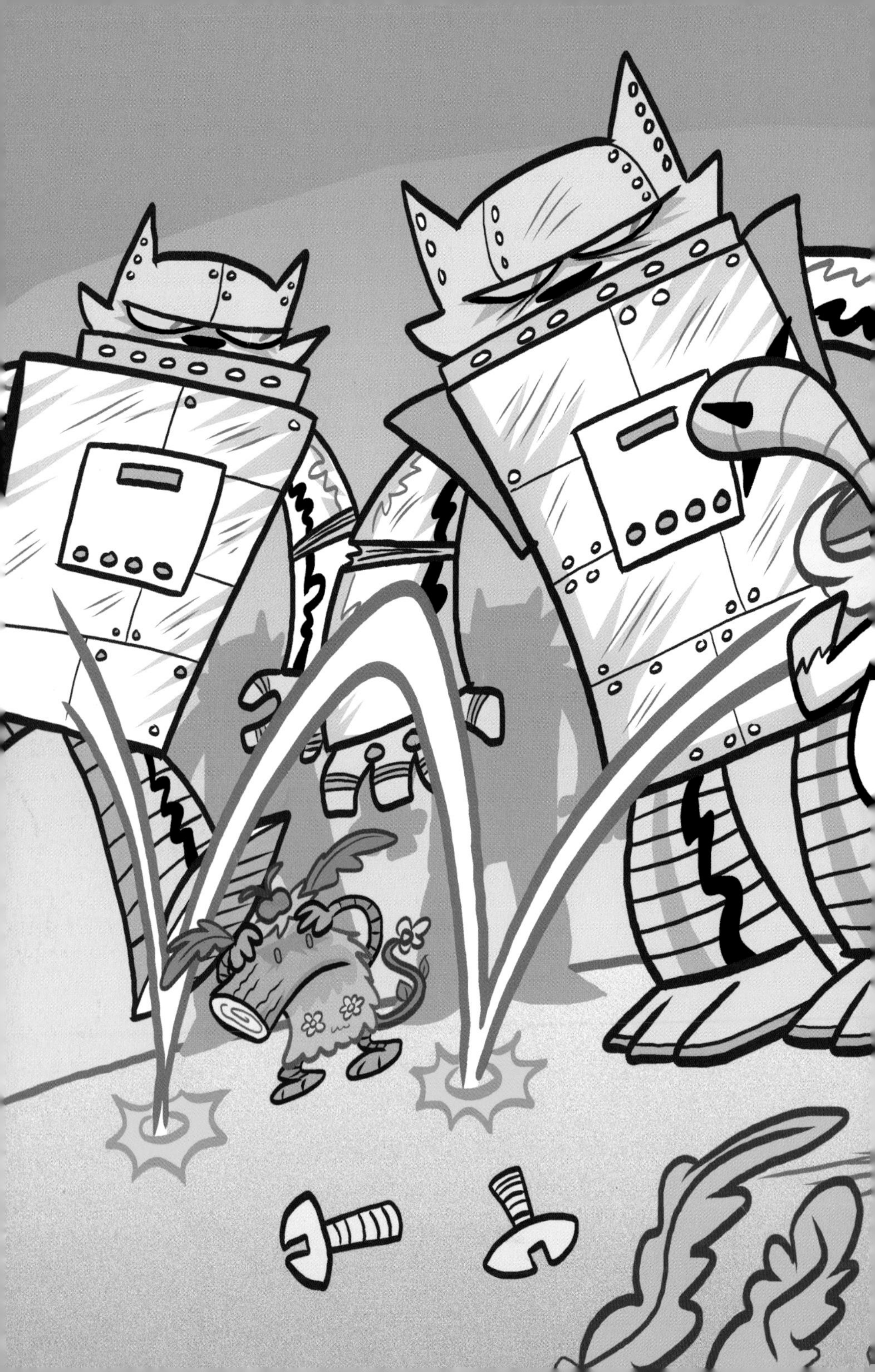

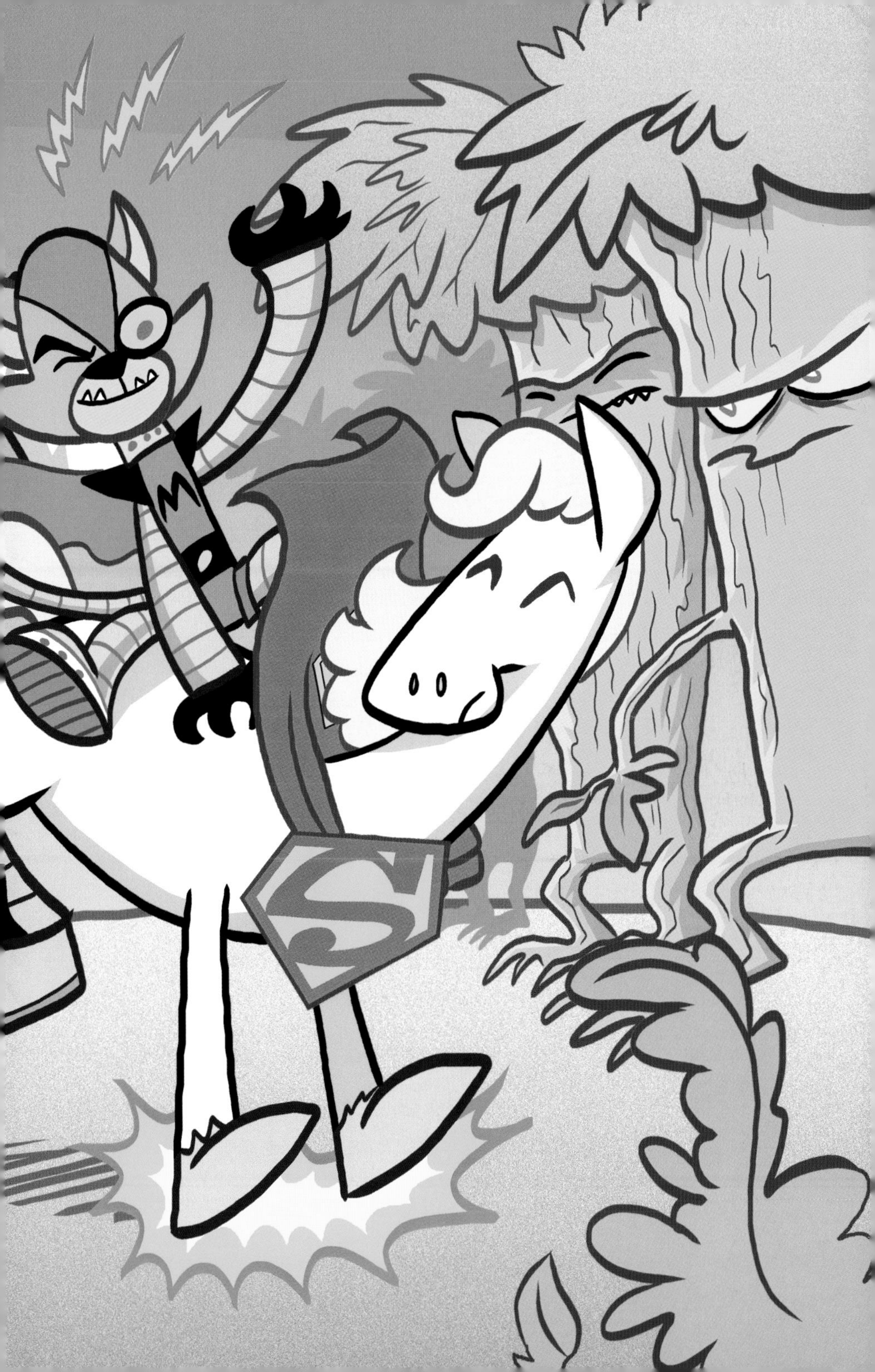

"**Neigh!**" Comet reared and bucked.

He tried to shake the bad kitty off,

but Mechanikat's claws were in deep.

Snorting and whirling, Comet finally

tossed Mechanikat. The villain fell to

the floor with a **THUD!**

Chapter 3

SECRET WEAPON

Slowly, Mechanikat rose with a screech. He was through playing games. He was ready to get out his secret weapon!

Mechanikat opened a door on his chest. **He pulled out a rock of green kryptonite from a secret chamber.**

The Super-Horse gazed down at the green glowing rock and snorted. He knew exactly what it was and how it worked. Kryptonite weakened Superman, Supergirl, and others from the planet Krypton.

However, Comet had not been born on Krypton! He wore the same colors and had many of the same powers as the Kryptonian super heroes. But Comet had gotten his superpowers on Earth. This glowing green rock didn't harm him at all!

Comet laughed at Mechanikat's secret weapon. The cyborg snarled back, confused. The Super-Horse lowered his head and stepped closer to the cat.

"Why isn't this working?" the evil cat yowled. He tossed the kryptonite away. Then the villain turned to where his Feline Fighting Force was being prepared in the factory. Ready or not, he needed them to work . . . now!

"Attack!" Mechanikat screamed at the cat-bots. **"Pounce!!"**

At that moment, the factory exploded with light. Dogwood had flipped the switch.

"Game over," Dogwood barked.

The lights showed rows and rows of cat-bots. They didn't attack Comet. In fact, they could not move at all.

"What have you done?" Mechanikat screeched.

Dogwood stood back and gazed at his work. He'd made his plant workers complete one more task.

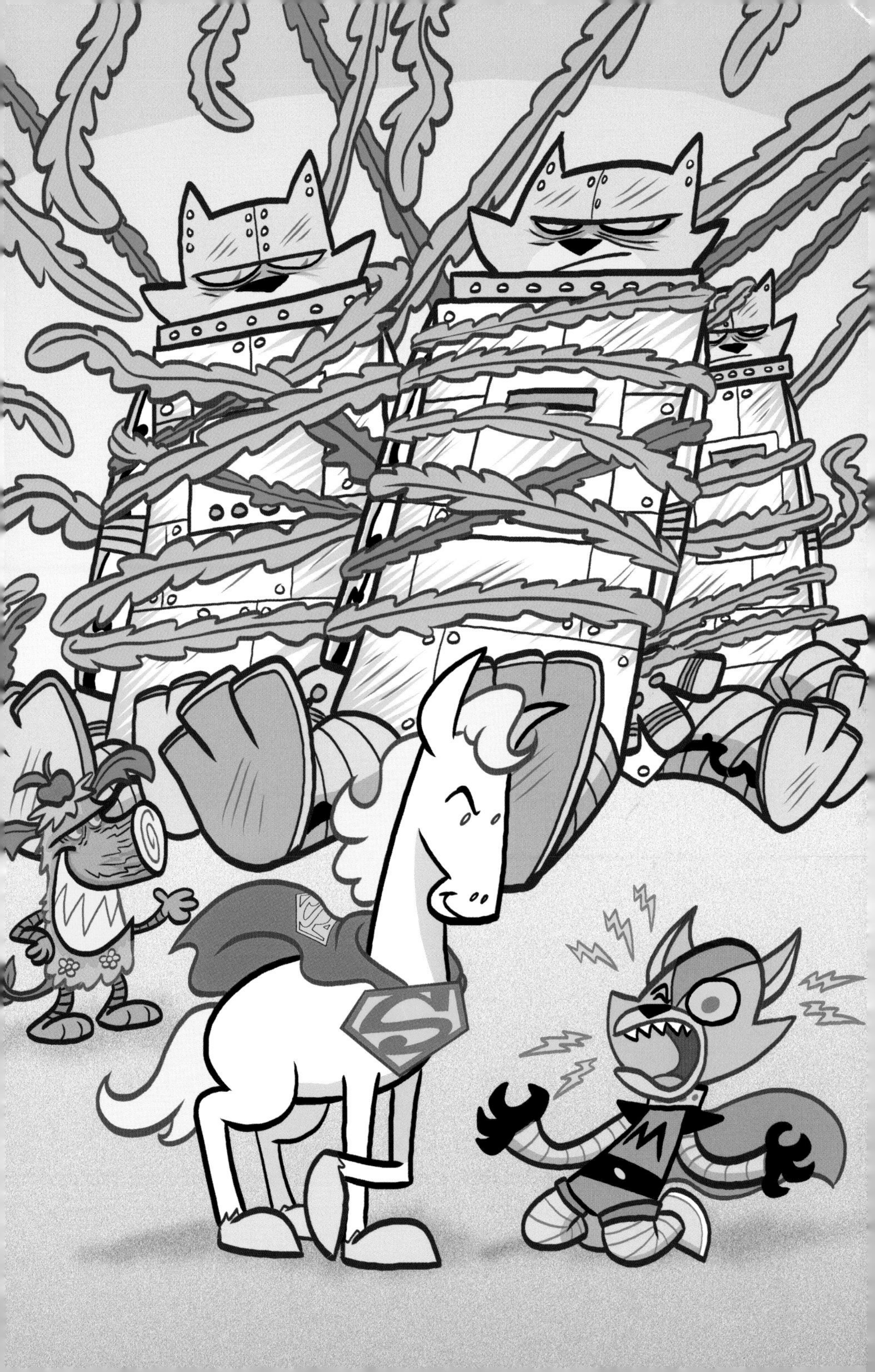

The grasses, vines, stems, and leaves had grown in and around the Feline Fighting Force. The cat-bot army was rooted to the floor forever.

"Reeow!!" Mechanikat yowled.

Dogwood bared his teeth and glared at the cyborg. "I'll teach you to lie to me," he said with a snarl. Then he chased Mechanikat out of the factory.

Comet chuckled. He could not wait to tell his friends about this adventure.

From the sky, Comet could see

Dogwood chasing after Mechanikat.

"You better run, you lazy double-

crosser," Dogwood snarled. "My bite is

much worse than my bark!"

KNOW YOUR HERO PETS!

1. Krypto
2. Streaky
3. Beppo
4. Comet
5. Ace
6. Robin Robin
7. Jumpa
8. Whatzit
9. Storm
10. Topo
11. Ark
12. Hoppy
13. Batcow
14. Big Ted
15. Proty
16. Gleek
17. Paw Pooch
18. Bull Dog
19. Chameleon Collie
20. Hot Dog
21. Tail Terrier
22. Tusky Husky
23. Mammoth Mutt
24. Dawg
25. B'dg
26. Stripezoid
27. Zallion
28. Ribitz
29. Bzzd
30. Gratch
31. Buzzoo
32. Fossfur
33. Zhoomp
34. Eeny

 1
 2
 3
 4

 5
 6
 7
 8

 9
 10
 11
 12

 13
 14
 15
 16

 17
 18
 19
 20

 21
 22
 23
 24

 25
 26
 27
 28

 29
 30
 31
 32
 33
 34

KNOW YOUR VILLAIN PETS!

1. Bizarro Krypto
2. Ignatius
3. Rozz
4. Mechanikat
5. Crackers
6. Giggles
7. Joker Fish
8. Chauncey
9. Artie Puffin
10. Griff
11. Waddles
12. Dogwood
13. Mr. Mind
14. Sobek
15. Misty
16. Sneezers
17. General Manx
18. Nizz
19. Fer-El
20. Titano
21. Bit-Bit
22. X-43
23. Dex-Starr
24. Glomulus
25. Whoosh
26. Pronto
27. Snorrt
28. Rolf
29. Tootz
30. Eezix
31. Donald
32. Waxxee
33. Fimble
34. Webbik

1

2

3

4

5

6

7

8

9

10

11

12

13

14

15

16

17

18

19

20

21

22

23

24

25

26

27

28

29

30

31

32

AW YEAH, JOKES!

Where do big cats go to exercise?

Dunno.

The jungle gym!

What did the pony say when it fell down?

Not sure.

"I've fallen, and I can't giddyup!"

What do you call a cat with eight legs?

What?

An octo-puss.

WORD POWER!

cyborg (SYE-borg)—a being that is half animal and half machine

Fortress of Solitude (FOR-triss UHV SAHL-uh-tood)—the secret headquarters of Superman

investigate (in-VESS-tuh-gate)—find out as much as possible about a crime or other event

mechanical (muh-KAN-uh-kuhl)—operated by a machine

obedient (oh-BEE-dee-uhnt)—does what he or she is told to do

villain (VIL-uhn)—an evil person or animal

MEET THE AUTHOR!

Sarah Hines Stephens

Sarah Hines Stephens has authored more than 60 books for children and written about all kinds of characters, from Jedi to princesses. When she is not writing, gardening, or saving the world by teaching about recycling, Sarah enjoys spending time with her heroic husband, two kids, and super friends.

MEET THE ILLUSTRATOR!

Eisner Award-winner Art Baltazar

Art Baltazar is a cartoonist machine from the heart of Chicago! He defines cartoons and comics not only as an art style, but as a way of life. Currently, Art is the creative force behind *The New York Times* best-selling, Eisner Award-winning, DC Comics series Tiny Titans, and the co-writer for *Billy Batson and the Magic of SHAZAM!* Art is living the dream! He draws comics and never has to leave the house. He lives with his lovely wife, Rose, big boy Sonny, little boy Gordon, and little girl Audrey. Right on!

ART BALTAZAR says:

Read all of the DC SUPER-PETS stories today!

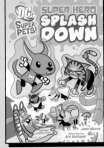

THE FUN DOESN'T STOP HERE!

Discover more:

- *Videos & Contests!*
- *Games & Puzzles!*
- *Heroes & Villains!*
- *Authors & Illustrators!*

@ www.capstonekids.com

Find cool websites and more books like this one at www.facthound.com Just type in Book I.D. 9781404864795 and you're ready to go!

Picture Window Books™

Published in 2012
A Capstone Imprint
1710 Roe Crest Drive
North Mankato, Minnesota 56003
www.capstonepub.com

Cataloging-in-Publication Data is available at the Library of Congress website.
ISBN: 978-1-4048-6479-5 (library binding)
ISBN: 978-1-4048-6846-5 (paperback)

Summary: Mechanikat and Dogwood team up to rain four-legged fury upon Earth. Only one foal can foil their evil plans . . . Comet the Super-Horse! This Stallion of Steel won't stop until he's corralled the crazy critters and protected the planet.

Art Director & Designer: Bob Lentz
Editor: Donald Lemke
Creative Director: Heather Kindseth
Editorial Director: Michael Dahl

Printed in the United States of America in Stevens Point, Wisconsin.
022013   007180R

DC™

SUPER-PETS!

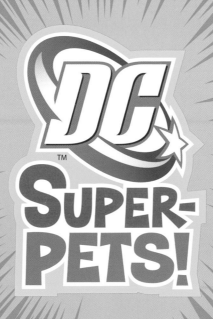

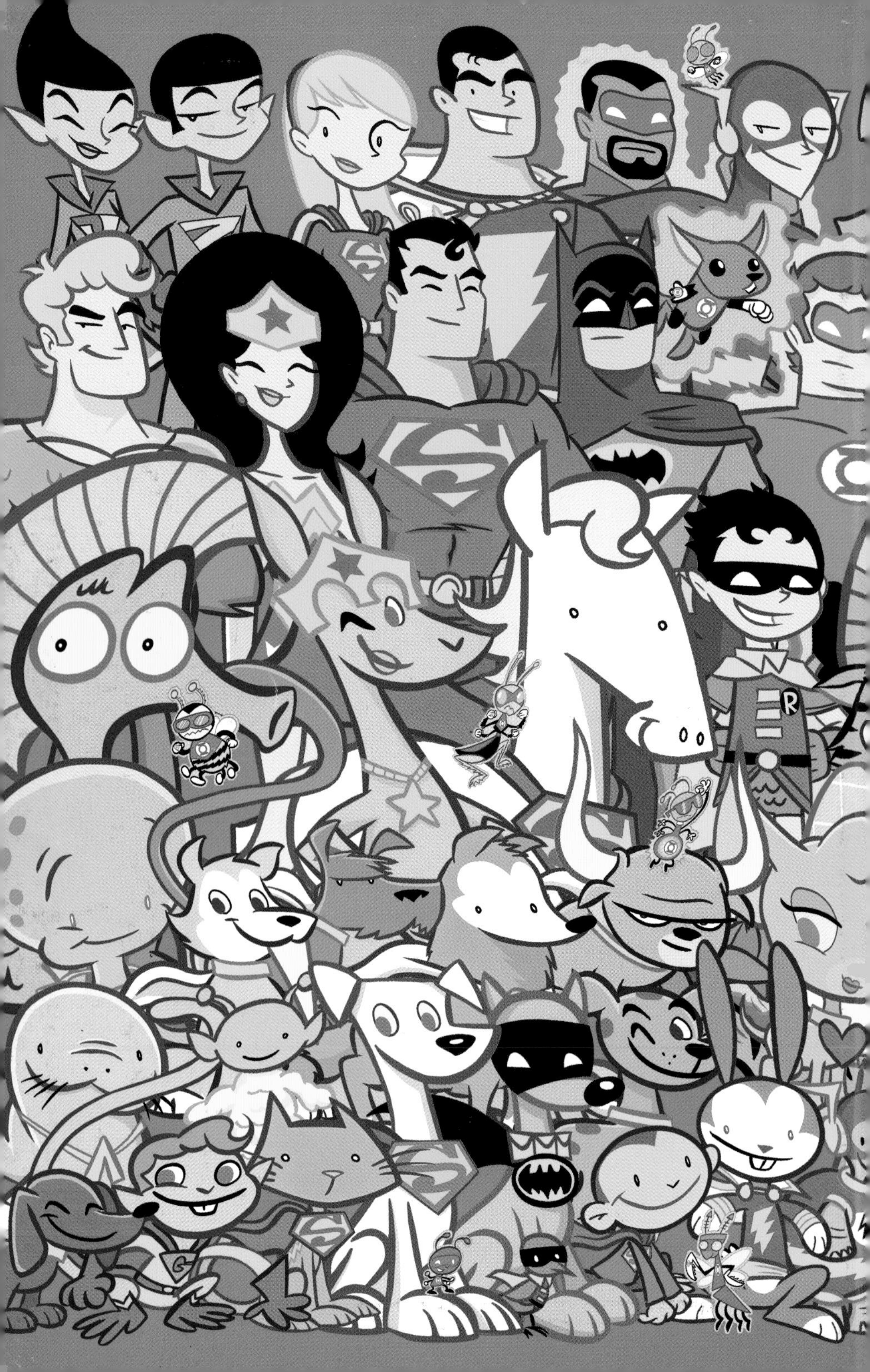